CRACKING THE CODE

A HEROES COLLECTION SHORT STORY

ALEXANDRIA BLAELOCK

BlueMere Books
MELBOURNE, AUSTRALIA

For permission requests, please contact enquiries@bluemerebooks.com.

Ordering Information:
Discounts are available on quantity purchases. For details, contact orders@bluemerebooks.com.

Cracking the Code/Alexandria Blaelock
paperback ISBN: 978-1-925749-70-0
digital ISBN: 978-1-925749-71-7

Book Layout © BookDesignTemplates.com

CRACKING THE CODE

It was what passed for morning on a day when you've been forced to take some of your annual leave.

That is to say, about lunchtime, but I had no idea what day it was, and there were no cues like garbage trucks, Australia Post guys on motorbikes, or flocks of brightly coloured school children walking down the street.

I did know that I didn't want to be on "vacation."

I hadn't taken one for years, so despite my protestations about how essential I was, they gave me a three-month sentence.

No excuses. Hand over your laptop and don't even think about contacting anyone at the office.

There was nowhere to go, and nothing to do, and I stayed up late watching the shopping channel and blockbusters made during the war and shortly after, and falling asleep on the couch.

It had been two weeks, and already the house looked like a bomb had gone off.

Not sure what it is about holidays that makes you use every single mug and plate and dish in the house before you wash the dishes.

There's a similar equation for the inner layers of your clothing, but not so much for the outer. I'd worn the same track pants and faded fleece since that first weekend.

And I couldn't have said for sure whether I'd combed my hair or not.

I was pretty sure it had been at least a week since I last showered.

I don't want to know what the mail guy who dropped off the package thought as I stood bleary-eyed and blinking in the daylight to sign for it.

Unemployed layabout at worst, at Death's door somewhere in the middle, or working shifts at best.

Or, in a way that was indefinably worse, not even worth thinking about.

The package sat in the middle of my table, half-hidden by layers of used tissues, junk mail, takeout chopsticks and napkins.

I think there might have been a pair of shoes on there too, and that ought to have made me feel bad because shoes on the table are supposed to be bad luck.

Not that I'm superstitious in general.

And I can't imagine how my luck might get much worse.

Touch wood.

The table is at least wood. Not very good quality, and not very attractive, but certainly wood. It's dented and scarred through living with me for twenty years.

The first dent came when I dropped a wine bottle on it; thankfully full so it didn't break.

I didn't have to open it; I knew exactly what was inside it. I'd found it on the train last Summer. Worn out from scans and a cancer follow-up clinic at the hospital.

It was a nicely laminated hardback notebook, with the cover of a lurid romance - all bright blue sky, blond woman with heaving bosoms clenched to the bare muscular chest of Mr Tall, Dark and Handsome.

The kind of old-fashioned romance where he punishes her with a kiss on page 16 and spends the next hundred pages relentlessly bullying her into marriage.

And for some reason, she says yes, perhaps because he gaslighted her into thinking she couldn't do any better.

Along with the book, there should be a myki ticket, a fifty dollar note, and a few store receipts.

I'd dropped it off at the police station about six months before, hoping the detectives could find the writer of the journal it contained.

It had been written by a young woman, whose boyfriend might have gone through abusive and out the other side to potentially life-threatening.

A lot like the romance the notebook's cover evoked.

Or it might have been a fake.

Six months was plenty of time to investigate, so it seemed safe to assume they hadn't found anything, because they sent the book back to me and its owner clearly didn't walk out with it.

I made coffee and took it out to the deck to drink.

The trees stirred in a light breeze and spattered loose raindrops onto the deck. There was no sign of the restless flocks of parrots that roost in the ones behind my house.

Oscar, the cat who'd adopted me at the old place, sauntered out behind me tail in the air and played nonchalantly with leaves blown in by the wind.

He at least seemed to appreciate the extra time I was spending at home.

The air was cold against my face and neck, so I pulled the hood of my fleece up. The cold was invigorating, though it made the inside of my house too warm by contrast.

I wondered if I'd overridden the central heating again.

I would not survive another eleven weeks of this if I didn't do something.

"Uh, Miz Jones?"

I whipped around to see a man leaning through the garden gate trying to get my attention, and I had the sense he'd been calling me for some time.

He was about my age, which is not as old as my white hair would suggest, (the unhappy consequence of my hair falling out during the first attempt at a cancer treatment).

Unlike me, he was dressed in jeans and a polo shirt that looked to be clean, and he glowed with youth and vitality. Which annoyed me about as much as being caught *déshabille* in my own backyard, and I went a bit feral.

"What do you want? What are you doing in my yard?"

Which seemed to amuse him, as if he'd heard stories about the monster, finally met her, and she was everything he'd imagined.

Now that he had my attention, he felt comfortable opening the gate and walking up to the edge of the deck.

"My grandfather tends your yard, I'm here today in his place."

That changed things a bit.

I moved closer to the edge.

"What happened? Is Frank okay?"

The boy grinned at me, "It's just a sprain, he slipped in the bathroom. He'll be fine."

"That's a relief. I take it Alda is taking good care of him?"

He laughed, "he wanted to come here to supervise to get away from her."

I smiled.

To be honest I felt a little jealous.

When I was recovering from the cancer treatment, I had been alone.

Though at the same time, I'd wanted it that way. I can't stand it when people fuss.

Frank had stopped by more frequently than he ought to bring me soup and tiny meatballs, and those little biscuits with jam in them.

And then I realised; the last time Frank had been here, he'd talked a lot about his newly single grandson...

And I might have mentioned my upcoming leave, and possibly the long and completely unscheduled days ahead of me...

All alone.

Abruptly, I became aware that I hadn't spoken to anyone in days and the idea of going back into that house on my own was weirdly horrifying.

"Are you Jed?"

He leaned an elbow against the stair rail, "yeah, how did you know that?"

I snorted, and not in a cute way.

"Any reason you can think of that he asked his computer engineer grandson to take care of my garden rather than, say, his construction grandson?"

"Oh, they've all got other things to do."

"The curse of the freelancer do you think?"

He shrugged, "I don't have any urgent deadlines."

I was pretty sure Frank had not met with any bathroom misfortune.

It was way more likely this was just his sledgehammer subtle way of matchmaking.

But.

He'd caught me in a weak moment.

"Would you like to come in for some coffee?"

Jed looked at me and rearranged his body against the stair rail.

I think he'd just figured out he was the honey trap.

Or I was.

Hard to tell when other people are doing the matchmaking.

"Ahh. Maybe I should just get on with the gardening."

I shrugged a shoulder and let the hand with my empty coffee cup drop, "suit yourself," and walked back inside.

At which point I realised how lucky an escape that was, given the state of the house.

And when I thought about it, me.

Not going to work ought not to be such a drama.

Putting Jed out of my mind, I took a shower and washed my hair.

I hesitated about whether to dress up or down, and eventually went for jeans, and a black button-down shirt. I rolled the sleeves up to pretend I was going to do some work of one kind or another.

And then I tidied and vacuumed, and when I opened the door to take the rubbish out, I ran into Jed just as he was about to knock on the door.

"Oh, the money!" I said, "hold on and I'll get it."

I dropped the rubbish bag on the floor and turned away.

"I'm sorry if I offended you before."

I paused, with my back turned, "no, not to worry. Frank said you'd just broken up with your girlfriend—."

Oops.

Open mouth A, insert foot B.

I looked up to the ceiling for a moment, trying to think of what to say or do, and ended up pretending that last comment hadn't happened.

"Wait here and I'll get your money."

I took a step, but he leaned through the door to grab my arm and stop me from walking away, "no. I mean..."

He dropped my arm, "is your offer of coffee still on?"

"Oh," I said, tucking a stray lock of hair behind my ear, "um," then "ah."

Way to go Gemma. So smooth.

At least I'd tidied up in the meantime.

"Let me just," I turned back to see him depositing the bag in the bin.

"Sure. Come in," I said to his back, but I left the door open as I walked back down the hall.

Lord knows what I was thinking.

That I was lonely.

That he was another human.

Who perhaps thought he had a female body to cry against.

And when I got back to the kitchen, I saw the package from the police service on the table.

Addressed to Miss Gemma Jones.

I hate it when my mail is addressed to my full name.

I picked it up.

The young woman who wrote the journal was obviously weighing on my mind.

And I had eleven weeks on uncommitted time, I could make an effort to find her.

Though did she want to be found?

Perhaps if I plotted out the places she mentioned, I might find a pattern in her movements.

It doesn't really matter how private you expect your journal to be, bits and pieces of identifiable fact slip through. Especially when you use it to manage your business.

Like maybe client names, fragments of copy or design.

"Nice place you have here."

I had forgotten about Jed.

How embarrassing.

I dropped the package back on the table, tucked my hair back behind my ear and moved through to the kitchen area to put the coffee machine on.

He picked it up, and gave me an eye, "what's the statute of limitations on Miss?"

"That's one of those things I hate about being an Anglo. If I lived almost anywhere else, I'd be promoted to Madam by now."

He grinned.

And then it occurred to me, I needed a team.

On those private investigator shows, there's always a computer guy. You can tell he's the computer guy because he (or she) is always wearing glasses and looks like he (or she) couldn't run one hundred metres if his (or her) bus was pulling away from the kerb.

I took a gamble.

"If you had to find someone when you didn't know their name, how would you do that?"

"Well, first, I'm not that kind of engineer, and second, what other information do you have?"

I pulled a chair from the long edge of the table out and gestured for him to sit in it. Then I opened the package and gave him the journal.

He flicked through it while I explained, "I found this journal on the train and handed it in to the police, but I'm guessing they haven't found the writer."

The coffee machine gurgled its last, so I made two mugs. "Milk and sugar?"

"Hmm? Oh. Yes, and no."

I made the changes and put the mug on the table in front of him before taking my usual seat at the head of the table.

And tucking my hair behind my ear again

He took a sip of his coffee, "well, the first thing would be to put your scruples aside and read it carefully for clues."

I rolled my eyes, "what are you? Like twelve?"

He put the book down, pulled himself to his full height, and rested his folded hands on it. "I'll have you know I read every one of the Hardy Boys adventures, and Nancy Drew as well. I know a clue when I find one."

I struggled to keep a straight face, but a smile leaked out nonetheless.

He held the book by the spine, and shook it, then investigated the pocket at the back to discover the myki, cash, and receipts.

He pushed the myki aside, "there's no point tracing that because if she was looking for a new start, she'd move somewhere far away from where she'd lived previously."

I smiled a little; after a quick flick through he'd reached the same conclusion as me; that the writer was female.

"Are you sure, she might have family nearby?"

"Okay, what would you do in that situation?"

I thought about it for a bit.

"I will concede I'd move away, maybe interstate, but I don't have any ties to bind me."

He frowned, "well, if she's gone interstate that'll make it harder to trace her.

"What about the cat?"

"The cat?"

He put his coffee down and swivelled in his seat to look at me, "this cat," and he pointed down at Oscar who was purring and rubbing his face on Jed's jeans.

"Ah. That cat. I'd take him with me."

Jed leaned down and scratched Oscar under the chin.

I guess he'd made his point.

"Why don't you read through the journal again, and I'll search for the stuff?"

I know I'd been thinking of him as "my" computer guy, but I hadn't imagined him wanting to get involved. And even if I did, I hadn't expected him to start right away.

Which led to the awful confession, "I don't have a home computer."

"No problem, laptop's fine."

I had a sense of where this conversation was going, "I don't have one of those either."

He stopped, stunned into motionless, "you don't have any kind of computer at home?"

"Well, there's an ancient tablet I use for ebooks, but it's been ages since I had a computer that wasn't owned by my employer."

"No wonder you're going nuts here on your—"

Perhaps the conversation between him and his grandfather hadn't been exactly the matchmaking one I'd been thinking it was.

That Frank thought I was going a bit nuts felt like a betrayal.

I turned my back towards Jed, only there was nowhere to go; it was *my* house, and walking away defeated the purpose.

This was exactly why I don't have a lot of friends, and don't invite them in. Once they're here, they leave thought and memory traces that can't be eradicated.

But I started walking in the direction of the front door, and when I got there, I opened it, stepped out and just kept walking.

He caught up with me halfway down the street and fell into step.

"Look, I'm sorry. I didn't mean to hurt your feelings; the words just slipped out. Frank's worried about you."

"I don't need your pity. Or his. I'm fine on my own."

My eyes were watering, and it was taking too much energy to hold them in.

I'd blame it on the drugs, only I was transitioning out of them.

I stopped walking and couldn't prevent myself from leaning towards him. He didn't move away.

Not matchmaking, I reminded myself, babysitting.

I straightened up and started walking back towards my house. If he couldn't catch me, I'd lock him outside.

And of course he could catch me.

"Ok, so maybe you don't need or want my help.

"You can go down to just about any electronics, computer or department store and for about a grand you can get a reasonable laptop with a good battery life, a display good enough for games or streaming, and a fairly good-size memory.

"I'll leave it with you."

And rather than follow me into the house, he watched me walk through the door and shut it.

I heard his car drive away.

And ridiculously, almost immediately wanted him to come back.

And then I told myself to get a grip on myself and sat down with the notebook, and my own journal to make notes.

I tucked my hair behind my ear.

First, I reviewed the store receipts. Stationery, storage boxes, lunch. Were they expense receipts? Were they from her old place or her new? I started a new page in my journal and noted the dates and locations.

And then I remembered I had an old Melways map book, so I started mapping them out to see if some kind of pattern might show itself.

I skipped over the contents, long-term to-dos and miscellaneous list pages of the book, and went straight to the calendars.

The monthly and weekly calendars were marked with stickers folded around the edges of the pages, so I flicked through to the first and checked the dates looking for appointments, deadlines, and to-dos, and where possible the locations.

The first month noted hair and a doctor's appointment. And as I flicked through the following months, a grant application deadline, a half-day seminar, an online workshop, a short story deadline, and so on until I had a reasonable list of dates that might lead to some viable next steps.

Then I skimmed through the daily pages in between, and these included meeting notes, voice mail transcriptions, and the girl working through issues that bothered her. That yielded even more clues for my notebook.

I snorted recalling Jed's self-righteous defence of his amateur detective skills.

Though I guess I had to give him credit for coming up with the same search parameters as me.

And then it occurred to me, that the diary might record information that could identify the violent boyfriend, so I skimmed through it again to make a note of those details.

By that point, it was clear to me she was a virtual assistant, so from that point of view, she could relocate anywhere in Australia. Though the fact that she seemed to specialise in an Australian context didn't mean she couldn't work anywhere else.

While I thought about what I'd learned, I changed back in to track pants and an oversize fleece, (clean this time), and as my hair had been giving me the shits all day, pulled it back into a ponytail.

Thinking I should really get it cut.

I wasn't real keen to get messed up again any time soon, so I cleared up the mess I'd made with Jed, emptied the dishwasher and put the two mugs inside.

Was it only that morning?

As I tossed the envelope the book came in across the kitchen to the recycling bin, something fell out of it.

It was a short note, indicating the detectives had not found any evidence of foul play, and therefore the case had been closed, and the book returned to me.

Well, of course they hadn't found any evidence - the journal didn't record any serious injuries. Not to mention that it ended before any serious assaults occurred. But if you read between the lines, she'd been terrified by the time it ended.

Clearly, Police Officers require a higher evidentiary standard than I do, but did they even look?

Or was that perhaps why the Police Officer I'd handed it to had given it back? Though with her impressively impassive face, she hadn't seemed unduly concerned at the time.

Had things changed? Had she been less than satisfied by her male colleagues' treatment of the matter?

And as he'd been involved, I wanted to test the idea on Jed.

Basically, because there was no one else.

It was a good excuse to call him, though somewhat less of a good excuse to call Frank and ask for his number.

Especially given that whole going a bit nuts thing.

The sky was darkening by this point, and I judged it was a reasonable hour to take a glass of wine or two before considering what takeout to order for tea.

And then it occurred to me that I was still going to the hairdresser I used to go to when I lived in the old place.

The one that took me two trains and an hour to get there, and two trains and a bus to get back. That I continued to take a day off every time I visited because the idea of having to explain my hair to someone else was exhausting.

I went back to her journal, and checked the dates - it spanned about four months. I checked my list of dates and appointments, and there were two hair appointments at the same place.

And it looked as though she might be about due another.

Could it really be that simple?

The main problem being, that I relied on public transport, and didn't own a car. I suppose I could hire one, but it'd been a long time since I'd driven anywhere.

Did I dare ask Jed?

All rightie, I'll admit it. I was starting to obsess just a little bit about Jed. He was kinda handsome in a tanned, dark-haired way, and he had a kinda confident, easy-going way about him.

But it was probably the drugs, because transitioning out of them substituted one set of issues for another.

At least until they're out of your system altogether.

So, yeah.

Probably the drugs.

I opened a nice bottle of Cabernet Sauvignon and left it to breathe while I got a glass and some Roquefort and crackers to eat with it.

And my phone so I could check the app to work out the best way to get to the hairdresser.

At which point, the doorbell rang.

It was Jed.

"Ah. I'm sorry to bother you again."

"Just come in, there's a lot to discuss."

He opened his mouth, then shut it again.

I left the door open and walked down to the kitchen to get another glass.

He shut the door and followed me down, depositing a laptop on the table.

"I felt bad about the computer thing, so I brought this old one of mine you can use."

I snorted as I filled the glass and handed it to him.

"Cheers," I said as I sat in my usual seat.

He echoed me and took the one he'd used before.

"I think I've worked it out."

He raised an eyebrow at me, and I laid my hand on the book.

"And your conclusion?"

"She used the same hairdresser twice in the book, and if that's a repeatable pattern, might be due another appointment."

"Ah, of course. What do you want to do now?"

I took a sip of wine, "I think I have to visit the salon to see if they know who she is."

"Where is it?"

"Heidelberg."

He took a sip of wine and looked at me for a bit. "Want me to take you?"

I couldn't help but smile, "would you?"

And he smiled back, "I surely would."

The next day, he arrived about eight in the morning, and we drove out to the hair salon, timing it for a little later than her appointment might start.

He waited outside while I went inside.

"This is a bit of an odd request, and you don't have to tell me, but can you look up who had an appointment at 9am on September 10, and again at 9am on November 5th last year?"

The woman behind the computer looked at me oddly, but looked the appointments up, and said, "the same woman for both."

"Okay good. Can you look and tell me if she has another one soon?"

She gave me a hard look, and said, "yes."

"Right. That's good too. I have something of hers, and I'd like to give it back."

She looked over my shoulder, and I wondered if she was looking at someone in particular, or was searching her memory for something.

"There's a coffee shop around the corner, why don't you go get a coffee and I'll call her."

I smiled, "thanks, that would be wonderful. It's her journal."

She nodded, and I turned away, resolutely not looking at any of the women in the salon.

"Do you want me to come with you?" Jed asked.

"Maybe in the same place, but not at the same table?"

"Good idea."

We ordered coffees, and while I waited, I got out my journal and wrote about what was happening.

It wasn't long before a youngish blonde woman with foils folded up in her hair, and a hair salon cape around her shoulders came in.

She clearly knew who she was looking for, as she approached me and sat down without hesitation.

"You have something for me?"

All very cloak and dagger.

"Why don't you tell me what you think it is, and I'll tell you if you're right?"

"It's a hard-covered journal with an old romance cover picture on it."

And that seemed enough, so I took it out of my bag and put it on the table.

She looked at it for a while.

"Are you okay?" I asked.

"You made me realise how easy it is to find me."

"Can't be that easy, the Police didn't find you."

She sighed, "I've changed everything else, but I couldn't let go of my hairdresser. It's such an easy tell."

"Only for those who know who she is."

"Well, if you, a total stranger found me, it would be a cinch for someone who knows me better."

"I hope you find someone kinder, and more respectful."

Her eyes brimmed with tears, and I had no idea what to do or say to make her feel better.

"I should go. I hope we don't meet again," and she took the journal and left the cafe.

Jed picked up his coffee and came across to my table.

"I think we made it worse."

He patted my hand. "Better to know now than to think she was safe until her ex turned up."

I sighed, "then why don't I feel better about this?"

"You should be proud of yourself. You solved a mystery and gave the girl fair warning."

I looked at his stupid smiling face.

But I *had* done that.

In the ugliest possible way, I had made her safer.

THE END

ABOUT THE AUTHOR

 Alexandria Blaelock writes stories, some of them for *Ellery Queen's Mystery Magazine* and *Pulphouse Fiction Magazine*. She's also written four self-help books applying business techniques to personal matters like getting dressed, cleaning house, and feeding your friends.

She lives in a forest because she enjoys birdsong, the scent of gum leaves and the sun on her face. When not telecommuting to parallel universes from her Melbourne based imagination, she watches K-dramas, talks to animals, and drinks Campari.
At the same time.

Discover more at www.alexandriablaelock.com.

BOOKS BY ALEXANDRIA BLAELOCK

SHORT STORY COLLECTIONS

The Histories of Hayward Hall
Lovelorn, Lovestruck and Love at First Sight
Common or Garden Variety Heroes
Case Files of the Wilkinson Detective Agency
Unavoidable Fates
Christmas Travesties
Five Faces of Felicia Clarke

OTHER FICTION

That Love Nonsense

MS BLAELOCK'S BOOKS

Stress Free Dinner Parties
Signature Wardrobe Planning
Holistic Personal Finance
Minimally Viable Housekeeping
Planning a Life Worth Living